The Mountain, the Desert, and the Pomegranate
Stories from Morocco and Beyond

Vanessa Paloma

The Mountain, the Desert, and the Pomegranate
and the Pomegranate
Stories from Morocco and Beyond

Gaon Books

Gaon Books
P.O. Box 23924
Santa Fe, NM 87502

www.gaonbooks.com

Library of Congress Cataloging-in-Publication Data

Paloma, Vanessa.
The mountain, the desert, and the pomegranate: stories from Morocco and beyond / Vanessa Paloma. p. cm.
ISBN   978-1-935604-03-7 (Cloth) (Acid-free paper)
        978-1-935604-16-7 (Paper) (Acid-free paper)
1. Morocco--Fiction. 2. Mediterranean Region--Fiction. I. Title.

PS3616.A356M68 2010
813'.6--dc22
2010017380

Manufactured in the United States of America.

The paper used in this publication is acid free and meets all ANSI (American National Standards for Information Sciences) standards for archival quality paper.

British Cataloguing-in-Publication data for this book is available from the British Library.

Art and Design by Gloria Abella Ballen
Cover Photo Vanessa Paloma

To my son Davidcito
David Zvi Hart, the sweet strong soul, who teaches me
about the holy mischievousness needed to pierce
seemingly sealed boundaries of separation

Contents

Introduction

The Mediterranean is a rich tapestry of opposites. Living in Morocco I experience life in circular and spiral time instead of linear time. Every day lived on these sun-baked lands is filled with elation and frustration.

When I first told people I was writing a book of stories, I felt strange. I am a professional singer and researcher—my writing has been for journals, newspapers, ezines and books on music and prayer. Actually, I did not really tell people at first. It was my own inner secret—I would sit and write at my computer overlooking the great expanse of the city of Casablanca and stare out at the infinite Atlantic Ocean. The stories came—some from memories, others from experiences, yet others from undiscovered inner worlds.

Why did I have the chutzpah to write fiction? How could I take my private creative outlet into the public eye?

One day I was talking about writing with a group of Moroccan women writers, and I realized that the Romances that I have been singing for years are short stories—jewels from a specific time and place. These songs are the memory-bank of the Judeo-Spanish community, the stories of life itself.

In *The Mountain, the Desert and the Pomegranate* I am telling my own stories, and they are not in song format. But of course, because of my life in song, I am comfortable in the world of stories.

I like to tread the invisible line between tangible reality and other realities. These stories are about the multiple universes that are encapsulated in the reality that we see and feel with our senses. We may only see one reality, however, there are many realities that we can experience when we are open to them.

Travel is one of the ways that helps me access different ways of thinking that allows suppleness of thought. Seeing new sights, hearing news sounds, words, smells, cuisines, traditions, even the difference in the light in various parts of the world can impact our perceptions. The light in Tangier is clear and blue, similar to Los Angeles. Grass in Colombia's Andes Mountains is a green I have never seen anywhere else.

Speaking many languages also opens the door to simultaneous multiple perceptions. The way one's mind works when a word is rolling on the tongue is a reminder that experience is different from one language or culture to another.

Saying the same word in various languages creates multiple relationships to the object in reference. Chair, *silla, chaisse, kursi, kisé*: (English, Spanish, French, Arabic, Hebrew), but does the chair change with each word? Or, is each word elucidating semantic references to the chair accessed differently in each language?

We are used to have direct, linear relationships to reality. Opening our minds and really sensing different ways of living while maintaining a rooted connection to one's own people, identity and culture can feel like an impossible paradoxical exercise. Maybe that is why it is so difficult for peoples of the world to make peace with each other.

The Mountain, the Desert and the Pomegranate is about paradox-holding. Try to encompass something and its opposite at the same time. We can, but it stretches us almost to the edge of ourselves. I invite you as the reader to try it with me.

Vanessa Paloma
Casablanca, Morocco
November 2010

Introduction

The Mediterranean is a rich tapestry of opposites. Living in Morocco I experience life in circular and spiral time instead of linear time. Every day lived on these sun-baked lands is filled with elation and frustration.

When I first told people I was writing a book of stories, I felt strange. I am a professional singer and researcher—my writing has been for journals, newspapers, ezines and books on music and prayer. Actually, I did not really tell people at first. It was my own inner secret—I would sit and write at my computer overlooking the great expanse of the city of Casablanca and stare out at the infinite Atlantic Ocean. The stories came—some from memories, others from experiences, yet others from undiscovered inner worlds.

Why did I have the chutzpah to write fiction? How could I take my private creative outlet into the public eye?

One day I was talking about writing with a group of Moroccan women writers, and I realized that the Romances that I have been singing for years are short stories—jewels from a specific time and place. These songs are the memory-bank of the Judeo-Spanish community, the stories of life itself.

In *The Mountain, the Desert and the Pomegranate* I am telling my own stories, and they are not in song format. But of course, because of my life in song, I am comfortable in the world of stories.

I like to tread the invisible line between tangible reality and other realities. These stories are about the multiple universes that are encapsulated in the reality that we see and feel with our senses. We may only see one reality, however, there are many realities that we can experience when we are open to them.

Travel is one of the ways that helps me access different ways of thinking that allows suppleness of thought. Seeing new sights, hear-

9

ing news sounds, words, smells, cuisines, traditions, even the difference in the light in various parts of the world can impact our perceptions. The light in Tangier is clear and blue, similar to Los Angeles. Grass in Colombia's Andes Mountains is a green I have never seen anywhere else.

Speaking many languages also opens the door to simultaneous multiple perceptions. The way one's mind works when a word is rolling on the tongue is a reminder that experience is different from one language or culture to another.

Saying the same word in various languages creates multiple relationships to the object in reference. Chair, *silla, chaisse, kursi, kisé*: (English, Spanish, French, Arabic, Hebrew), but does the chair change with each word? Or, is each word elucidating semantic references to the chair accessed differently in each language?

We are used to have direct, linear relationships to reality. Opening our minds and really sensing different ways of living while maintaining a rooted connection to one's own people, identity and culture can feel like an impossible paradoxical exercise. Maybe that is why it is so difficult for peoples of the world to make peace with each other.

The Mountain, the Desert and the Pomegranate is about paradox-holding. Try to encompass something and its opposite at the same time. We can, but it stretches us almost to the edge of ourselves. I invite you as the reader to try it with me.

Vanessa Paloma
Casablanca, Morocco
November 2010

Contents

Earth and Sky

I was born to a man who came from the world of the earth and a woman who came from the world of the skies. They wandered the earth in search of their happiness and dreams, but for me, it was a test to live time and time again in a new place, making new friends, learning a new language and a new culture. We lived in the mountains surrounded by loving family, then in the tundra surrounded by snow, on an island surrounded by sea and mango trees, and then in the mountains again. I started to sing and make music. Books were my best friends, and my life was one of having fun expressing myself with stories and songs.

One day my parents decided to move to the land of the earth, and I was grown-up already and didn't want to go. I stayed for a time, but in the end I went to be with them, and I suffered a lot in that land. I couldn't learn the ways or understand the people until I went to college where I found people that were more like me.

Later, I moved to the city of light. Although the city was exciting, I felt lonely and lost, and I found that in my loneliness my family memories loomed larger and larger in my thoughts. I was fascinated by past traditions in our family that had almost died but now were coming back in full illuminating force.

With this fascination growing inside, I traveled to the land of dreams and learned a deep wisdom that opened a door for me to learn the secrets that defined who I was as a soul in this world.

When I returned to the city of light, I came knowing who I was, not the one I had tried to learn in so many different places. I had a voice that grew from within and grew and grew. This voice expressed all the voices that had been quiet for so many years, for generations.

The voice came, and I sang about light and dreams and earth and sky and tundra and mountains and sea, and all was ONE.

Part 1

The Earth

Cantigas D'Amigo and Coyotes

y friends from the California Institute for the Arts (CalArts) decided to have a black tie performance dinner party in the middle of the desert. It was late in the fall, so we weren't running the risk of it being too hot, and the rains still hadn't started.

The requirement for an invitation was that you perform something, and that you wear black tie or an evening gown with your hiking shoes. I drove up early in the afternoon from Los Angeles to Valencia passing the San Fernando Valley and climbing into the arid mountains. From there we went to the place where they had been building a formal dining table for the last two days on the side of the desert mountain.

It was a three-mile hike in from the highway, and I was glad to have brought my heavy hiking boots. California mountain desert plants are resistant, prickly and sturdy, and the gravelly dirt they grow in is hard and crumbly underfoot. I was carrying my medieval harp, and had a long black gown that hugged my figure and fell to my ankles. It was getting dusty on the bottom. I was concerned that my formal concert gown might be ripped by one of the plants as I hiked to this mountain in the desert.

The evening began with gaslights gracing the foot of the stage and the long table incrusted into the mountain wall. There were linen tablecloths, china, silver and crystal. Wine and large platters of delicacies had been prepared to accompany the desert performances.

The stars were out in their full splendor looking down at this original gathering of creative spirits. The sky was so clear and each star could be seen distinctly and brightly. The wind caressed our skin, bringing with it the different energies of the human hustle and bustle of Los Angeles and the silent strength of the high desert. Somewhat similar to the synergy we embodied that night: refined artistic performance in an unrestrained natural habitat. It seemed like a propitious evening for the encounter of opposites.

Fifteen people arrived. The men were in tuxedos and combat boots. There was a Boteroesque woman in a long flowing emerald silk gown and hiking boots. I thought it was magnificent that all these people had hiked three miles into the desert mountain in their fineries. I was thrilled to be a part of this artistic adventure.

A couple of singers began with an operatic duo. Then there was a boring comic. At least he was boring to me. I did not understand why his jokes could ever seem funny to anyone.

They asked me to sing. I had a little stool up on the makeshift stage, and I sat there to sing the cycle of seven *Cantigas D'Amigo*. These songs come from Medieval Iberia and are the largest body of female-voiced love lyric that has survived from ancient or medieval Europe. They were written in Galician-Portuguese, a language that doesn't exist anymore in our day. In these songs a girl sings as she's looking out to the Atlantic Ocean at Vigo, north of today's Portugal. She is looking out to see where her lover is, why he hasn't come back. She asks her mother when he will be back, and what to do in the meantime?

From the coast of Vigo to the Mohave Desert mountains there are oceans, mountains, valleys, cities, lakes, rivers and many, many people. Worlds, universes separate these two places. But this special night, while we were gathered under the desert stars these opposite places in the world had the potential to come together and kiss. A twenty-first century woman and a medieval woman could become one. Their yearnings, their hopes and their dreams were the same.

I sang the Cantigas and played the harp in one, then other, and another. Half way through the cycle of songs, the strangest thing happened. A chorus of coyotes joined me. As I sang and crooned out these despairing love lyrics in medieval Galician-Portuguese, the coyotes had gathered in a circle around us and howled joining in with my voice. When the songs were finished the coyotes' howls quickly died away, and there was silence.

Never before had I connected with wild animals through my music. It was exciting, as it was unnerving, and I wondered what had triggered the coyote chorus to join me in making music that night. Was it the girl's desperate love pleas from seven hundred years earlier? Or maybe it was something wild, raw, and deep in my own voice that I didn't even know was there.

(In the Mohave Desert Mountains of California, 1997.) 17

Lifting Up

I was finally there. I had taken the risk of leaving my job and deciding to move to Jerusalem for an open-ended stay with the support of a spiritual community from the City of Angels. The City of Gold and its many mysteries awaited.

I woke up before dawn that first morning because of the jet-lag I had from traveling halfway around the globe. I jogged down the street to the Haas Promenade—it was a garden built on the side of a hill full of olive trees and rosemary plants. As I arrived I saw a beautiful sunrise view of the Old City. The light was gleaming pink and yellow and shining off the golden dome, beckoning me to come close, behind the walls.

I could see the whole city from this vantage point to the south. I saw the Mount of Olives, the Dome of the Rock, the West Jerusalem and the hills surrounding it. It was a veritable golden, sandy, mysterious beautiful sight.

That day I decided to take the bus into the center of town and explore by myself. I dressed in my favorite jeans, the ones that fit me snugly and a cool vintage lime green shirt that showed off my figure. I had my comfortable platform shoes that I wore almost every day. The bus I had heard my friends talking about took me to a street bustling with activity. I saw most of the passengers getting off at *Mahane Yehuda*, the *shuk*. I got off too and explored through the fruit, vegetable and nut stands. People were jostling around with their many bags of groceries. The vendors were screaming out the names and prices of their fruits and vegetables in Hebrew. I was amazed to hear Hebrew in this kind of use, not just in a prayer. There were so many religious men with all sorts of outfits, hairdos and hats. I was intimidated by them, even scared about their possible hostility to me, the obvious stranger. I ordered a falafel sandwich from one of the vendors on the street.

After I explored the *shuk*, I wanted to go to the Old City to the Kotel, the Western Wall. That is where all Jewish pilgrims dream of going to put their prayers on a small paper and stuff it into the crevices between the huge ancient stones. Not knowing any Hebrew and traveling alone made it a challenge to find the right bus! I stood at the bus stop for a while and analyzed the different people getting on the buses. I thought I would take the bus that felt "right" and God would take me in the right direction. I decided to take one which was full of religious looking people.

The bus I took turned into a neighborhood soon after our departure from the street of the market. Gradually I found that I was the only woman left on this bus that was full of ultra-Orthodox men. What seemed to be a whole class of boys with side-curls got on the bus, and I started to feel more and more uncomfortable and out of place. The bus was veering away from the center of the city and headed into an ultra-Orthodox neighborhood. I was extremely self-conscious of the way I looked and felt eyes boring into me from behind. In a desperate attempt to save myself from getting deeper into this neighborhood I got off the bus and started walking. Here I was, in my tight jeans and screaming green shirt with platforms walking through an ultra-Orthodox neighborhood where all the women wear skirts and all the men look away when they see immodestly dressed women coming in their direction. I saw a couple talking across the street, and I shouted to them, where is the Kotel? They pointed in a direction, and I turned right and continued walking.

I walked down a long busy road hoping to reach the Kotel soon. My stomach started to feel queasy. I continued, hoping to see the Old City walls soon. I finally saw the city walls straight in front of me and discovered I was close to the Muslim and Christian Quarters. I was arriving from the northern side of the city. I finally entered the walled city through the Christian quarter. I started feeling sicker and sicker. As I arrived to Jaffa gate next to the Tower of David I sat down and tried to quiet down the discomfort in my stomach.

After talking to one of the vendors in Jaffa gate, I sat down to calm my stomach and thought I was getting better. I looked around at the intense activity: a man with a barrel of freshly baked bread for sale, older Palestinian men sitting in the café across from me, taxis entering through the gate bringing curious tourists into the Old City, restaurants, signs beckoning you to come explore bazaars and shops. At one point the discomfort overtook me, and I threw up into the moat of the Tower of David Museum. What a disaster my trip to the Kotel had turned into! I had to call my friends to see if they could pick me up and take me back because I had no idea how to get back to their apartment. I was in no state to explore my way back to my bed.

On the way home I was forced to open the car door more than once to throw up on the street. The falafel from the *shuk* was my downfall. My friends said it was the remains of the Diaspora getting flushed out of my system. Jerusalem was purging me of extraneous remains from other worlds.

That night after I ate crackers and sipped hot tea I went to bed. As I was falling asleep, I felt a wind over my body. I had a clear vision of myself dressed in a flowing white dress. I was in a domed room standing and looking up towards the balcony of a smaller room. This small room was to the left of the larger room. I felt myself being quickly lifted and saw myself floating to the top of the dome with my white dress hiding my legs and feet.

I actually physically felt a wind over me, and an actual elevating from where I was lying in bed. Now I was ready to go to the Kotel. I had done whatever purification was necessary before I was able to go pray at the Wall.

(Inspired by real events that happened on January 1998 in Jerusalem)

☙❧

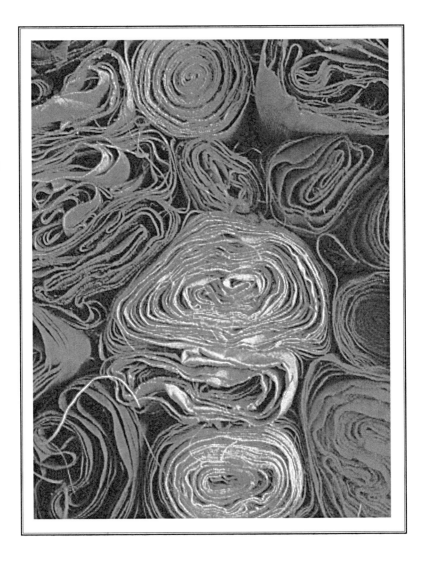

La Mantilla

In my early origins I was on a black bolt of silk. I was woven in Spain in the nineteenth century. I was one of twenty bolts of silk that were bought by a struggling merchant in Seville. He decided to stock silk in different colors since it had become the latest rage for ladies to each own their own embroidered mantilla. His plan was to get out of debt by selling many meters of silk to cover the shoulders of fashionable women throughout Spain, Portugal and what was then known as Spanish Morocco.

Since I was buried deep in the middle of the bolt, it took some time for me to finally be up for sale. I would lie patiently rolled up on the bolt of cloth, squeezed next to all the other material that was also waiting to be unrolled and sold. For us, raw pieces of material, our life started when we turned into a real thing that people used, either to wear, look at or decorate their home.

But in the meantime, I watched and waited.

When I was still just silk threads, I was soaked in a color fixative made from water and vinegar. The dye was in a big stinky vat, full of a boiling hot black liquid made of iris roots and oak galls, which ensured an ink black color. I (if you could call me I yet since I was just a bunch of separate strands of silk thread floating around in a vat of liquid) stayed in there overnight soaking to the darkest black. Then I was washed and dried in the scorching dry sun of Southern Spain. After being in those vats full of hot and cold liquids, the sun, the dryness and the wind felt great.

I enjoyed the moment my threads were woven together, one pushing tightly up unto the other making me feel more and more whole. The loom pushed in one direction and the tightening instru-

23

ment came and pushed me in the other direction making my strands closer and closer together. The more I was tightened, the better and stronger I became.

Finally, I was rolled up into a bolt of thirty yards length and stacked together with a roomful of bolts of all sorts of different colors, patterns and materials.

One morning a distinguished older man came into the shop and asked for ten yards of black silk. He was in Seville on a business trip from his native Tetuán, Morocco. He was dressed in the European style, but his Spanish had a distinctive accent that I recognized as Haketía, the Judeo-Spanish spoken by the Jews of Morocco. This Spanish was a mix between Old Castilian, Hebrew and Arabic, and I had heard this hybrid language before because many people had come into the shop from Tetuán. This city at the northern tip of Africa on the Mediterranean Sea sounded like an interesting place!

You can imagine my excitement when I realized that I was going to be in those ten yards of black silk that he was buying! Now my lethargic wait on the bolt was finally over, I would travel, and turn into something real and then see the world while I was decorating some young or older lady's shoulders. Or so I imagined.

The merchant cut the ten yards of silk, wrapped it all into a neat package which he tied with a jute string and off we were, to the next stage! The older gentleman, Sr. Jacobo Garzón, walked out into the busy street with his packet tucked neatly under his arm. Later, he put the package inside a trunk, and I couldn't really see what was happening. I could hear things, feel movements and sometimes smell pungent smells. This became a new way to gather information about my surroundings.

A couple of days later I felt something that was reminiscent to my days in the dying vat, a swish, a movement...we were on a boat! His business in Spain must have finished, and we were heading towards Tetuán on the Strait of Gibraltar. I was bursting with the anticipation of arrival on another continent. Seeing different architecture, smelling different spices and hearing the music and voices of Morocco.

We weren't on the boat for long. Not even overnight. I didn't realize that Spain was so close to Tetuán. Now it made more sense that there had been so many people coming into the shop from this famous city in Morocco. We disembarked at the port of Martil, which was at the foot of the mountain where Tetuán was located. I felt us travel up the mountain, and then through some noisy crowded streets called *El Ensanche*, the Spanish part of the city.

Mr. Garzón lived in the *judería*, the Jewish neighborhood inside the old city. From inside the packet, of which I formed a part, I felt us going inside the *medina* walls and start the labyrinthine walk into the heart of the *judería*.

When we finally arrived to our destination, he knocked on what sounded like a large thick ancient door. I heard a creaking sound and we were inside. It seemed quieter and cooler inside the house. Three women's voices were excitedly greeting him, and they sat down to eat a small snack before he opened up the gifts he had brought from across the Strait.

I was bursting with anticipation to know who would be my mistress. I had waited long enough sitting on that bolt in that little store in Seville! I was ready for my adventures to start! I was ready to go to parties, afternoon teas and weddings. I was ready to be caressed by the hands of my owner and to cover her shoulders and grace her head with my beautifully woven threads.

Fortunately the women were just as excited to receive their gifts, as I was to know whom I would belong to. Right after they sat at the table Mr. Garzón opened up the packets. He opened up my packet first to show them the beautiful ten yards of black Spanish silk. When he opened up the paper I was wrapped in, I took in the scene around me.

We were in a spacious room with high ceilings. There were arched doorways going out into the courtyard, which had beautiful plants growing up trellises. The cool tile floors had some muted red woven carpets with geometric designs. There was a sitting area and a dining area. There were beautiful colored tiles on the walls. The furniture was sober and elegant in dark woods.

The three women were actually one woman of around 40 years old and two young ladies of fourteen and sixteen. It must be the mother and her daughters. I later found out the mother's name was Fortuna Garzón and the two daughters were Estrella and Hana. The two girls were of marriageable age by Jewish community's standards in Tetuán at the time. This black silk was to make each one of the women an embroidered mantilla. This would be part of the girl's trousseau.

My mistress was Hana, the sixteen-year-old girl. She was studious and a real thinker. She liked to do things with her hands, and she decided that she herself would embroider flowers on the black silk with black silk thread. She also later added an ornate lace trimming all around me. I liked the feeling of her hands on me when she worked on the embroidery. She would occasionally pull the work away to take a look at it, admire how far she had advanced, and then continue. This would take place along with her sister and mother and other women who would gather to sing, gossip and make marriage matches around afternoons of embroidery.

Soon after I was completed, embroidery, fringe and all—I made my first public appearance on her shoulders one late afternoon when we went to her friend Luna's house.

It was that fateful afternoon that Hana's life changed. The man she was to marry had just arrived from America looking for a bride to go back with him. He was staying at Luna's house because he was her cousin from Portugal. But he wanted to marry a girl from Tetuán and take her to America! I heard that afternoon that this was quite strange. Most of the men left their brides in Tetuán, went to America, made their fortune and then came back. But this man had been in America already and wanted to take his bride with him! The young woman he married would be quite lucky to have such an adventure, but she would also face the difficulty of being alone in a far-off land. This couldn't be any simple girl. She would have to be resourceful, independent and mature.

His name was José Machado. He was twenty-eight, tall, with a dark brown moustache, and he wore a hat. When he walked into the room where the women were gathered talking about him and his quest for the right woman, they all fell silent immediately. He was very gracious, cracked a couple of jokes and left the room—not before locking eyes with Hana, whose heart somersaulted.

That was it. I knew it would be Hana. Yipee! I was excited about the prospect of taking a transatlantic steamer, of crossing the miles of deep ocean and arriving to the land of dreams. Who would have known that sitting on my bolt of cloth for so long would have such a reward of traveling and adventures?

It took them a lot longer to realize that they were meant for each other, and her parents were concerned to find out about his background. His family had left Morocco for Portugal fifty years earlier with a whole group of Jews looking for better fortune.

When they finally started talking about engagement, Hana seemed excited too, but very frightened of leaving her family behind. She knew it would be a world that was completely different from hers. Her mother and her sister would miss her terribly, and the prospects of coming to visit were very slim. It would most possibly be a farewell.

I sat folded in a trunk for the weeks it took us to cross the Atlantic Ocean. Once again I had memories of the dying vat, and now added to it, the experience of our boat ride across the strait of Gibraltar. This time it was a lot longer. It was dark in the trunk, and I was pressed up against the other silks, linens and cottons Hana was taking as her wardrobe to America. I heard them saying we were going to Panamá. I wondered what I could expect in Panamá. I was sure it would be quite different from the narrow winding streets of the *judería* of Tetuán.

Panamá turned out to be quite humid and full of trees and gigantic plants. The first time I went out on Hana's shoulders I saw that the city was small, but it had some large avenues, and was built more like *El Ensanche* in Tetuán than the *judería*. There were many kinds of people in America! Even some of the faces looked like nothing I had ever seen. There were also people in different kinds of dress. Some women had mantillas, but only a few. I was definitely a sign of distinction for my mistress.

José had left the business with his partner while he was gone. During the eight months he was in Tetuán things had taken a turn for the worse. I could sense their tension. They were newlyweds trying to establish a new home in a far-off land, and their business had taken a sudden downturn.

There was another couple in the small Jewish community who was planning to move to Colombia. They started talking to José, telling him what their cousin in Boyacá (a department in the mountainous region of the country) was telling them about the fabulous business opportunities in that place. They planned to start shipping goods from the interior of the country to the coast. The plan was to move to a small city called Sogamoso high in the Andes Mountains, a place rich in mining.

During the two week trip from Panamá to Sogamoso I went back into the trunk, pressed up against my new friends, the other clothing!

In Boyacá there were many superstitions about the nature spirits that controlled human's destiny. But of course, Hana, being Jewish from Tetuán, had her own set of beliefs. Throw salt into a glass of water when you've had a bad dream, she would tell her husband. They would sleep with a pair of scissors under their mattress to cut any negative spirits that would disturb them in their sleep.

She would go out once a week on market day and walk through the *plaza de mercado* where local peasant women with long black braids sat on the ground behind their goods. They had burlap bags and baskets filled with carrots, potatoes, yucca, plantains and all sorts of fruits and vegetables. These ladies sat in the cool mountain air covered by a *pañolón*, a black-fringed woolen shawl, quite different from me, a silk mantilla. I am much finer and more delicate. The *pañolón* was more practical, to warm them up while I am a Spanish Mantilla, a fashion and status statement, elegant and beautiful.

Hana had a daughter after the first year of their lives in Soga-moso. They named her Rebecca. She had very large eyes that looked longingly into the distant space. Hana wrote her parents a letter tell-ing them about Rebecca's birth. She was wearing me when she wrote them, maybe because I was a direct link to her family and environ-ment back in Tetuán. When she wrote the letter she cried and cried, tears of loneliness and longing. Even though her husband was very attentive, and she was happy to have little Rebecca, Hana missed her family terribly. The raw mountainous beauty of Boyacá had some things in common with Tetuán , but the people were very different from the Jewish community she had known growing up.

Then, tragedy struck. Hana's husband died suddenly leaving her a young widow with a child in a land she hardly knew. As she con-sidered going back to her homeland, she received word that both her parents had passed away when a deadly virus blew through Tetuán. She heard that the *judería* was not be the same with so many of her family members gone. There were too many memories, and it would be too difficult. Her sister had married and left the country, moving to the city of Lisbon. Without a place to go, she stayed where she was in the house that she knew.

Hana would wear me on special occasions, and sometimes just on days when she wanted to connect to Tetuán . Soon, Rebecca start-ed asking her mother to let her try me on. It made me so happy to see the sparkle in the young girl's eyes when her mother would describe the way she had embroidered the flowers and added the lace. Soon Rebecca was learning to embroider too!

Hana and Rebecca decided to move to a larger city of Tunja where the Jewish community would be more active. In Sogamoso there were a few Jews, but they were losing their connection to the ancient traditions. Most men had married locally since it was very rare to find a Jewish woman in this land. More than once Hana was asked to marry again, but she always said no.

We stayed for some years in Tunja the capital of province. One day, Rebecca wore me when she was invited to a very special dinner

29

in the house of the *Fundador de Tunja*, and I saw amazing paintings of fabulous animals on the ceiling of the dining room! The painter had painted an animal from Africa, a rhinoceros that had a strange armor-looking skin and a horn out of his nose! What a strange animal! Tetuán was in Africa, but it did not have animals like that. I think Rebecca also thought of Tetuán every time they mentioned Africa and its mystery and wonder. She had never been there, but she dreamed of going one day.

Rebecca grew up and married and moved to Bogotá, the national capital. It was the largest city I had seen. She had a daughter and two sons: Ana Inés, Joaquin and José. By a strange twist of fate she was also widowed young, but she remarried quickly. Her mother, Hana, continued to live with her, and she took care of the three grandchildren. She would cook delicious cakes soaked in sweet wine like her mother had done in Tetuán, and she told them stories of her childhood in that faraway land.

Years passed, and I was in the closet more than out. Mama Hana was older, it was difficult helping with the three children. She wasn't a young healthy woman anymore, and her own daughter, Rebecca, was trying to balance her life with her new husband who was not always ready to care for the children of a previous marriage.

We lived in a large house with three patios. The first one had a fountain and beautiful flowers, the second one had two fruit trees and some cooking herbs. In the last patio there were chickens and sometimes a turkey to be fattened up. When it came time for the turkey to grace the table, it would be taken to a butcher who knew the proper way of killing an animal.

One day sixteen-year-old Ana Inés had me in her hands. She was trying to copy the flower patterns on this mantilla to embroider on a mantilla of her own, but she was making hers in colors. She wanted something more modern, and not the black somber color of her grandmother's mantilla. Rebecca came in and introduced her to an older man who had traveled the world. He was an engineer who had studied in London and North America. He spoke

English and French. He was almost 40 and single. He was looking for a bride.

It was decided that they would marry. I felt her tears wet me as she cried every afternoon when she embroidered. Her real love was a young man named José who was her age. They were both young and knew their parents would never agree to this match. She bemoaned her bad *mazal* to have to marry this older boring man. Neither her mother nor her grandmother understood why she was so upset. I wished I could talk to her and tell her that I thought she was such a beautiful and creative young girl that she could wait and have any husband she wanted later.

But the day of the wedding was set, and I came out of the closet not to sit in Ana Inés' hands, but on Mama Hana's shoulders. I saw the whole ceremony and knew that Ana Inés' heart must be shrinking a little every second that passed. There were many photos and then they left on their honeymoon.

Mama Hana passed away soon afterwards. I went back on the shelf and imagined I would never see Tetuán again. She was the last link to the old country. Ana, who was now being called Ita, had four children, three girls and a boy. Every time there was a celebration for the birth of a child I would come out of the closet and sit on her shoulders—a connection to her past, her family and the happiness of her childhood. Ita continued embroidering, and she would pour out her desires, dreams and stresses into her needle. I was very proud of her skills and progress as an artist.

As fate would have it, Ita was the third woman in her family to become widowed at a young age. She had to work a great deal because her older-engineer husband, who was supposed to provide so well for her and their children, had left no plan for them after he passed from a cancer which devastated his body in a few weeks. The children were very good students, and all were able to study abroad and develop interesting and meaningful careers. Ita decided to pass me on to her youngest daughter Inés who was a painter, and the one she thought would appreciate my delicately embroidered flowers

31

the most. She wore me out on fancy and important occasions. Inés married an American professor, and they lived in Puerto Rico and Colombia for many years while I sat surrounded by mothballs. Inés wanted to preserve me and my link to the past, but she was afraid to bring me out, lest something happen to my delicate threads. Do mantillas get old too?! I thought this was funny but maybe true.

When their daughter grew up, Inés gave me to her. We went on many trips, and then a beautiful thing happened. One day we went on a long trip, and when we arrived and she opened the suitcase, I knew. We were in Morocco! I could smell it in the aromas of roses, cumin, azahar, and mint. I could hear the guttural Arabic words in the house and feel the soft ocean air. We were close to Tetuán. The sounds were louder, but the twisting lanes of the *medina* were filled with people negotiating the food for their families and the new mantillas for their shoulders. I wondered about these new mantillas, and the people who would wear them.

Now, I rest in a closet in Casablanca, and I come out on special occasions: weddings, circumcisions, and public appearances that Hana's great-great-granddaughter does. She brought me back to Africa, to Morocco, and sometimes even takes me to Tetuán. I leap for joy when I come out of the closet and drape her shoulders. Other people might not know how much I have seen and the strength I give to those who wear me, but my mistress knows, and she absorbs from my silk threads the memories and wisdom of Mama Hana, Mama Rebecca, Ita, and Inés. I hug her shoulders in her joy and in her sorrow in the magical land of Morocco that I first knew so long ago.

(Based on the origins and travels my Mantilla has made. She originally belonged to my great-great-grandmother.)

34

34

Shabbat Shalom
Madame Soulika

On the Shabbat when the weekly portion of *Lech Lecha* is read I went to Marrakesh. This portion tells the story of Avram, later to be known as Avraham, or Abraham--leaving his home, his family and everything that he knows to venture to the land of Canaan and start his destiny. He decided to abandon his land, his ways, his history and only when he started his voyage did the help he needed come.

I went to Marrakesh planning to spend Shabbat on my own in a small hotel close to *Djama el Fna*, "*La Place*" in the medina of Marrakesh. In this mythic square day and night there are snake charmers, veiled Berber fortune-tellers, story-tellers and musicians. In the evenings a platoon of food-stalls are rolled out, some specializing in fresh-squeezed orange juice, others in nuts and snacks, and others offer *harira*, one of Morocco's national plates made of chickpeas and tomatoes. Other stands offer steaming *tajine* and fried salty foods.

Since I was traveling alone, my plan was to buy kosher food from a local Jewish woman who cooked meals for passing tourists. I would stay inside Friday evening, and I was looking forward to a quiet evening on the terrace of my small *riad*, a family run hotel around an open courtyard, and I could look across the rooftops of Marrakesh and see the yellow glow of the city's lights at night. I might even see the smoke rising from the food stands at *La Place* and hear drums and the *Gnawa* musicians playing their high-pitched percussion for European and American tourists.

My goal was to simply spend a quiet and peaceful Shabbat in Marrakesh, so I could board a plane for London early Sunday morning. I was traveling to my nephew's Bar-Mitzvah, and Marrakesh-London-America was the cheapest flight I found. So, I took the Thursday night train from the northernmost tip of Morocco down to the rose colored city in the south, Marrakesh. As the train approached at dawn, I had peeked out the window, only to see mud huts and palm trees in a desert landscape. It was fall, the summer heat had abated, but it was too early for snow on the Atlas Mountains that surround Marrakesh.

I slept on one of the upper bunks of the orange sleeper cabins of first class. There were three other people in the cabin that evening. Two were Iraqi Kurds traveling throughout Morocco, who told stories of the horrors they lived through as adolescents during the attacks against their people by the Iraqi government. Now they lived in London. The fourth person was a flamboyant Spanish painter. He owned a little *riad* in the medina of Marrakesh in which he was painting colorful frescoes as it was being re-modeled.

When they left the train station the Iraqis, who spoke Arabic, were able to find a taxi easily and for a moderate price. I was left haggling in meager French with a taxi driver that knew I was foreign and was ready to charge me an exorbitant fare. The flamboyant Spanish painter materialized out of nowhere, scrapped together a sentence in his meager Arabic and got us a deal to share a taxi to *La Place*. He even told me that he knew of a great *riad* where I could stay. Since I was traveling to see my family, I had my largest suitcase, and it was bursting at the seams with presents from shiny slippers, gold encrusted leather notebooks, spices, tasseled keychains, and a special gold-thread embroidered box for the Bar Mitzvah boy.

I got a man to put my suitcase into a *carroza* the glorified wheelbarrows that are used to transport everything throughout the alleyways of Marrakesh. The *carroza* man was lugging this heavy suitcase through the tiny alleyways of the medina while I looked for a *riad* with the flamboyant Spanish painter. Every riad he recommended looked like a cockroach-infested dive. I would not settle for something that wasn't clean, quiet, beautiful and affordable.

After several minutes of turning blind corners in this maze of alleyways, we came to a man sitting on the ground with an incense burner. He asked me if I were married. He asked if I had children. When I responded no to both, he started waving the incense all over me and muttering a blessing in Arabic for my future *baraka* (blessing). He shook the incense over me, under me, around me, in front of me and in back of me! All the while mumbling and mumbling, chanting, and finally he put his hand out. After all *baraka* has a price.

I was somewhat taken aback by this encounter, but just afterwards I found the right riad to spend Shabbat. Maybe his blessing had actually worked. The flamboyant painter took off to his *riad*, and I prepared to go out to make arrangements for the evening and the next day, Shabbat.

I had originally planned to go to the synagogue in the new city for services where I hoped to meet Jewish people who lived in Marrakesh. But, it was far away, and it was already afternoon, so I headed toward the ancient Jewish quarter hoping to find someone in the old synagogue, which was closer. I had heard that they only had services during the week, but I was sure that someone would know how to find kosher food.

When I arrived to the synagogue a blind man who was there understood what I wanted and took me to the home of his aunt and cousin. We were led by a small boy to whom he spoke in a rough voice. Even though he couldn't see, he knew the way very well. We passed vegetable stands and shoemakers, spice merchants and even a small pharmacy.

The house we were looking for was hidden behind a small unassuming wooden door with large round metal nails forming a geometric pattern. We entered into a small chamber and then passed through a second door. Only then did we enter the courtyard where two large women were braiding copious amounts of hallah bread. One of them was older and had a handkerchief over her head, and the other one was younger with dyed blonde hair with dark roots.

I spoke little French and no Arabic, and they didn't speak English or Spanish. They did speak some Hebrew, as did I, so we were able to communicate minimally, enough for them to understand that I needed to buy food for Shabbat.

When they realized that I was traveling alone, they invited me to stay for lunch. Then, they told me that I should come to have dinner tonight and lunch the next day, and I could go to the synagogue in the *Mellah* with them. No need to venture into the new city, it was quite far to walk. When I told them I would come for lunch but not dinner because I didn't want to walk the streets of the medina alone at night, they understood, but they were still not satisfied.

They were distressed that I would spend Shabbat evening by myself in the *riad*, even though I had dreamt of the view from the terrace and the sights and sounds of the night. For them, being alone on Shabbat was a depressing thought, and they said no one should spend even part of Shabbat by themselves. After some discussion in French and Arabic they told me to bring my bags from the *riad* and stay with them for the whole Shabbat...and even to stay until Sunday when I was leaving for London.

I looked up to the sky from the courtyard and saw a stork flying lazily above in the blue square of sky that was visible from below. I felt as if time had stopped, and the stork reminded me of the slow rhythm I should allow myself to take more often.

I accepted their offer.

It was a bit crazy, I did not know these people. I would be completely vulnerable. What if something went wrong...but I decided to take the risk; the small nagging voice about possible negative outcomes was probably coming from unfounded fears.

I returned to the *riad* with the youngest son who took my gift-laden suitcase and dragged it all by himself through the streets of the medina, refusing any and all help from me. We arrived just in time to take a shower and wash off all the dust and the baraka-infused incense I had accumulated since the early morning train arrival in Marrakesh.

What I hadn't expected was that there was no shower in the house. There was no time to go to the *hammam* (the public bath) before Shabbat. So, I quickly bathed with cold water from a faucet in the small room off the courtyard which housed the toilet.

Madame Soulika, the older woman, lit for Shabbat with oil in a glass taken from the top of the armoire in the dining room, which held all the dishes. This room was a rectangular room lined in sofas with a long table placed in front of it. The table was decked with bread, wine, salads and fish. The women sat outside sipping tea on the sofas in the courtyard. They waited for nightfall when the men returned from the synagogue.

39

I gave a short Hebrew lesson to the eleven-year-old boy, and later he clamored *geffen, geffen¹* (wine, wine), so the meal would start. French, Arabic and Hebrew were going back and forth; tea, cookies, cakes and advice and anecdotes. There were only three Jewish families living in the mellah now, and this family was preparing to leave the country soon. Their blind cousin ate his food silently and Madame Soulika passed more and more food around. The boys were curious about me and asked question after question. "How could I travel alone? Was I single? What work did I do? Where was I going. Would they ever see me again?" I answered in Hebrew, and their mother translated as much as she could understand into French and Arabic.

After dinner they were sitting on the sofas quietly. Madame Soulika was caressing the nineteen-year-old boy's head as he reclined on her lap. The eleven-year-old boy and his mother were across from her, and the blind cousin stood by the large wooden door. The older boy started to softly sing Israel's national anthem in a song-whisper. I began to sing with him, and they all had tears in their eyes at that moment when they understood how even though we had no common language, we were a part of the same people; we had common feelings to share. In the heart of the Mellah of Marrakesh on a Shabbat evening, people from opposite corners of the world connected by the shining thread of a melody.

1   Shorthand in Morocco for Kiddush, the blessing over the wine said on Sabbath before the festive meal.

That night we all slept in the same room where we had eaten. They closed the two large wooden doors with five bronze latches from the inside. The iron-grated windows were also shuttered, and we were truly protected inside a dark enclosed room. We slept lining the walls. The beds were on the sofa-banquettes. Feet touching heads, heads touching feet. I had never slept in a room with a whole family of unknown people, in a city I didn't know, not speaking the same language.

The next morning the walk to and from synagogue was memorable. Everyone knew my hostess and spoke with her: the spice merchant with baskets full of aromatic and colorful powders, the tailor in his tiny shop, the drugstore lady taking a veiled woman's blood pressure...and men in *djellabas* wished us Shabbat Shalom as we walked through the alleyways in what felt like a time warp back 150 years. Then, we knocked on the outer door with the large brass ring, and the door opened and we were back inside the safety and quiet of the courtyard salon.

After lunch we spent the rest of the afternoon in the natural light drinking tea and talking with other women that came to visit from the community. I could see the birds flying overhead through the courtyard and the sun seemed to be hot, but we were protected inside the thick walls.

After the sun went down, we sat in the increasing darkness. They counted the three stars through the square framed by the courtyard walls to know that Shabbat had ended. Afterwards they served a delicious cereal-like soup that they make for every Saturday night.

Time stopped on this Shabbat inside that courtyard in a way I had never quite experienced before. Maybe I had to go away from my family, home, land and language to encounter a part of my destiny, just like Abraham did so many thousands of years before.

(Inspired by events that happened in the Marrakesh Mellah in October 2007.)

42

The Silver Coins

ne sunny morning the whole house was abuzz with movement. Twenty tables had been delivered the day before. One hundred chairs had arrived in the middle of the night from a nearby restaurant. Three maids had been in the kitchen cooking for five days. They had been preparing chicken wings, salmon pâtés, sweet meat pies, roasted lamb, freshly baked breads, salads with fish slivers, tiny pizzas, small fried fish, almond pastries dripping with honey, cakes and more.

This was the morning of the *F'kan Kohen*, the *Rehmido*, and the *Pidión HaBen*: the redeeming of the firstborn, our little son.

Thousands of years ago the Hebrews raised their first-born sons to a life of Divine service. The oldest sons of the family were the priestly class for the whole people. They say this is why the Jewish first-born babies survived the tenth plague before leaving Egypt. They were divinely consecrated.

A mother's first-born boy was consecrated to divine service, and a father gave his first-born son a double portion of his possessions as his birthright inheritance. It was also customary for a father to vow his first-born son to the study of Torah.

However, first-borns (*bechor*) lost their status as keepers of the Holy after the incident with the golden calf when the Hebrews were in the Sinai desert. They weren't patient enough to wait for Moses to come back down the mountain with the complete Torah. They had just experienced communal prophesy together on the mountain, but once Moses took a little longer than they calculated, they panicked. Only one of the twelve tribes did not participate in this calf-making. It was the tribe of Levi. After this the whole tribe of Levi took over the first-borns and they became the priestly class. Today they are called the Cohens and Levites.[2]

When the Jewish Temple was still standing the Cohens would do the service while the Levites accompanied the service with beautiful songs and music. Their prayers and study affected the consciousness of the whole Jewish nation. Since the Romans destroyed the Temple in 70 C.E., Levites and Cohens have had only a trace of their holy work left. Cohens do bless the Jewish people on different occasions with a special hand position that facilitates the flow of Divine blessing, and the Levites wash the Cohens' hands before they do these blessings.

My thirty-day-old son awoke early ready to eat. His grandfather from Casablanca was rushing out to do morning prayers and popped his head into the room and gave him a blessing: "May God bless you and keep you, may God shine His countenance upon you and give you peace." He was born with a good star and to receive a blessing the morning of his *Fkan Kohen* was a good sign.

Finally, the tables were all set; the buffet was laid out by the window facing the garden that was full of fruit trees. Pomegranates, dates, olives, figs, lemon, plum, grapes among others...and the sun came out this day, even though it was late in the fall.

The father redeems his baby when the child is thirty days old, by paying the money equivalent of five shekels "by the sanctuary weight." The mother must have given birth naturally to a son, this allows for her to redeem this baby, the first to open her womb. When it was no longer known what exact weight the five shekel coins should be, Jews used five silver pieces or five local coins as redemption money, or even a ring, a silver or pewter tray of clothing.

The grandmother from Marrakesh was giving orders in the kitchen and rushing upstairs to do her hair; the grandfather from the United States was furiously typing on his computer as he jotted down all the experiences in this tradition-rich culture; the grandmother from Colombia kissing the baby and taking care of me—did I have everything I needed? The grandfather from Casablanca was busy calling people,

44

---

2   Kohanim and Levi'im in Hebrew.

setting up tables, searching for the bag with the five silver pieces that were misplaced in the craziness of the tables, chairs and food.

The baby's father arrived in a suit with tennis shoes, a hip version of a younger generation Jew living in Morocco. I tried on a couple of outfits, settling on one that was a mix between elegant and artsy... most everything still didn't fit me even though the birth was one month ago...

And as always happens with these events...The guests started arriving even before expected. Then the frantic moments really began. The great Rabbi of Morocco walked in on his cane and so did other bearded rabbis with their wives, who had their hair covered with hats or wigs. Everyone was excited to see the little one. And the President of the Jewish community of Casablanca said he, during his eighty years of life, had never come to one of these ceremonies.

But, our son slept through all the excitement and was really quite peaceful even with one hundred people in the house crowding in to meet this new soul in the world.

The Moroccan grandfather had searched all over the city for special coins to redeem this little one. They were solid silver, antique Moroccan coins; silver pieces that had been used before Morocco's independence in 1956. They had the images of the Kings of Morocco, especially the King who saved the Jews during the Second World War. There were two coins; the oldest of all, that had the Jewish star, the Star of David. Jews were the ones that minted coins back then, and the six-pointed star was both on the silver pieces and also on the Moroccan flag. The French changed that; they saw a discrepancy in the six-pointed star being the official representation for Morocco. Unfortunately this was probably the beginning of the splintering of relations between Morocco and its Jews.

They had assembled the best *paytanim* from the city—these men sang liturgical poems in Arabic in the Andalusian style, and they all sat at one table and took turns singing one song after another. The baby slept.

Finally everyone was present, and the ceremony started. In Tangier they call this the *rehmido* which comes from the Hebrew word *Rehem*, the womb, the womb baby—the one who opened the womb. Why is it only for a boy and a boy who opened the womb? *Rehem* also connects to the Hebrew and Arabic word for compassion—*Rahman*. There is something about the womb of a mother that is full of compassion? Is it that this child, who is divinely consecrated has a special relationship to compassion? It could be that's why the first born are the ones who are supposed to do priestly work. Because they have an intrinsic connection to compassion from the fact that they opened the womb—*rehem*.

The Kohen asked me in front of everyone: "Is this your first child? Is this the first fruit of your womb?" After I said yes, he asked me to hand the child to my husband. The baby had no idea that he actually didn't belong to his parents but to the priestly class. This ceremony was a grand endeavor to buy him back and ensure that he did belong to us.

Then, the Kohen asked for the baby, and it was only then that I understood the gravity of the situation. Actually, the Kohen could decide to keep him! What a horrific thought. My throat constricted as my husband handed our son away. The Kohen explained the ceremony to the assembly, and as he asked my husband if he wanted to redeem the child. My husband's voice cracked as he answered yes, and the assembled community laughed. Was it a nervous laughter? Was it laughter of relief that they were not the ones experiencing this difficult moment?

When my husband handed the five silver pieces to the Kohen and received our son back in his arms, both he and I breathed more easily.

Even though today this ritual seems like a mere formality, it is not at all meaningless. If you ponder for one moment what it could mean that your child doesn't belong to you and that you have to pay for him and ask the grace of the Kohanim to allow you to have him... Oh, it is no wonder that mothers used to place all their jewelry on a tray with the baby to encourage the Kohanim to keep the jewelry and not the child.

But the tradition is that the Kohanim always returned the jewelry, money, coins etc—but they return it as a gift back to whomever gave it. So, really it's the Kohanim that come out best from this. They are able to show their generosity of spirit and how throughout thousands of years they have not taken advantage of the privileged position of being the priestly class.

At the end of the buffet that day, the Kohen ceremony, and the Andalusian singing in Hebrew, the people gathered with me in the red round Moroccan salon, and I sang the old Judeo-Spanish songs in honor of my son, who now finally, officially belonged to us.

47

(Inspired by real events which happened in Casablanca, Morocco on November 18, 2009)

Mysterious Trains

When I was a young boy we would travel by train to visit my Mother's parents in Tangier. They lived in one of the new apartment building complexes that had sprouted up around Tangier during the economic revival. After sixty years of virtual abandonment by the previous King, his son, the new King had invested in the north of Morocco, and the economy of the region had boomed. People loved him, and his picture was all over the city showing the different facets of his personality. The King as military man, the King as father, the King as religious cleric, the King as sportsman, the King on his throne...Tangier was enjoying this new relationship of proximity to the monarchy and its obvious economic benefits.

We lived in Fez and the difference between the two cities was burned in my blood. I breathed Fez, but I felt like flying in Tangier. There was something about the air from the two bodies of water clashing...the Mediterranean and the Atlantic Ocean meeting right there at the Strait of Gibraltar—it created a bit of schizophrenia in the mood of the true Tangerine.

If you looked in one direction you could see Tarifa, and the coast of Spain. Most Moroccans couldn't get a visa to cross the strait, even though one could see it with the naked eye. Sometimes there were young stowaways on the ferries that made the crossing. They would wait until the ferry was making its way back to Morocco and then they jumped into the water and swam into Spain. Sometimes they were caught by the strong undertow of the motor and killed. But others were lucky enough to survive and enter Spain unperceived by the port authorities.

The bay of Tangier and the calm waters of the Mediterranean were solace to those who chose to look in that direction.

If you sat at Café Hafa, where the Rolling Stones and Jimi Hendrix chose to smoke and drink tea, you would look in the direction of the waters of the Atlantic. It was a raw, strong and ferocious surf. The water was darker and more ominous...and there you looked out towards the infinite. Or, you could think that you looked towards America. Some Moroccans thought that was the infinite. It was the land of infinite possibilities, and infinite amounts of money.

I was drawn to the eccentric ways of people from Tangier, and was always excited when we traveled there. The trip itself already hinted at what the city had in store. There were always different kinds of people on the train to Tangier, different from the normal people in Fez. There were writers and artists and the occasional mysterious foreigner.

One time I was traveling in the first class cabin, and we had just arrived to the Sidi Kacem train station where we changed to the train to Tangier. The oil refinery across from the station soiled our very thoughts as we waited to catch the train from Casablanca. It bustled with hip young people and big city energy. They were different from those of us coming from Fez the mysterious, Fez the dusty, Fez the traditional.

Once on the train to Tangier, I decided to use the bathroom. By then, it was dark, and the light wasn't working. I didn't want to lock the door with it being so dark. I sat on the toilet, it was smelly of old urine and gas fumes with the smell of old wet metal—maybe the tracks? Or was it on my hands from touching the handlebars to climb into the train from the platform some minutes earlier?

The darkness flickered with the passing lights and there were brief snatches of moments where I could make out the mirror behind the door, the sink, and the whiteness of the toilet seat, all the while the tracks were loud underneath.

The train was moving fast and honking its horn as it rushed through the small villages. Many times I've seen boys my age throw rocks at the train, and then I hear the low thud against the metal of the car. On one such trip a rock hit the window just inches from my head as I napped, and the window exploded into a dense spider web of cracks, shocking me into wakefulness. Now, I am leery of sitting by the window.

I was in the dark toilet that night hearing the loud tracks racing underneath, lost in thought. I suddenly felt the door opening. I put my hand against it, so the person wouldn't enter. But they pushed harder and harder. Even though I was resisting, they were able to push into the bathroom.

I saw a young elegantly stylish woman who looked Moroccan, or was she? Something seemed amiss. She looked down as she prepared to enter the bathroom and when her eyes met mine as I sat on the toilet and peered up from the darkness, she let out a scream and turned back. She hurried away from the bathroom, which is at one end of the cabin. I ran out as I made up my pants and saw her turning again when she was almost at the other end of the cabin. The door closed behind her in the hallway…She was gone.

I was hoping to talk to her so she would feel it was OK, but I guess I must have really scared her.

This was the first time I remember a woman felt threatened by me. But I wanted her to understand that I wasn't trying to scare her. I had myself been scared to close the door behind me in total darkness.

(Inspired by a real event that happened on a train between Fez and Tangier, February 2008)

Part 2

The Sky

52

The Desert, the Mountain and the Pomegranate

The Desert is the Sahara. It is the largest desert in the world and runs across northern Africa, separating the people of the North from Sub-Saharan Africans. People who have very different languages and cultures.

53

The Mountain is in the Atlas mountain range in Morocco. It is a *Jbel* (Peak or mountain in Arabic) that soars high on the edge of the desert. It blocks the sandstorms of the Desert from coming into the rest of the land.

The Pomegranate is a special pomegranate that never dries out, and each one of its seeds has magical qualities. The pomegranate that was transported to the Desert and crossed the Mountain.

We all stood quietly waiting for the storyteller to tell us the whole story. Now that he had outlined the main characters in the narrative, we would understand what he was going to tell us next. The stories I heard during summer nights at *Djama el Fna*, in the heart of Marrakesh, were popular and improvised. Sometimes they had drums to punctuate the drama, or special lights. However, rumor had it this storyteller was different from the others, his stories changed people in a secret way.

Deep in the gleaming desert of the Sahara was a red juicy pomegranate with exactly 613 seeds. You should know that 613 is a special number, it adds up to ten, six plus three plus one, and ten is really one plus zero, which makes One. This is what our Rabbis taught us, this is the One of our Creator. In the variety and multiplicity within the fruit we are shown the unity of all of creation.

*Six hundred and thirteen is also the number of command-
ments that our Creator has asked us to fulfill throughout our
lifetime as Jews. I try very hard to fulfill all the commandments
that I can, but there are some, like the commandments surrounding the sacrifices at our holy Temple in Jerusalem, that I can't do.
Actually nobody can do them because the Temple in Jerusalem
was destroyed thousands of years ago.*

*I am a Berber Jew living on the edge of the Sahara. I live on a high
mountain that overlooks the sandy plain. My ancestors came from
Jerusalem after the destruction of the First Temple in the sixth century B.C.E. They crossed the sandy, hot desert on a trade route. Their
caravan traveled only during nighttime and early morning hours.
They were guided by the position of the stars in the night sky as they
crossed miles and miles of sand dunes. They guarded their skin with
light swaths of cloth draped around their bodies, head and face. This
protected them from the sun, the wind, the sand and the bugs. They
ate dates, figs and nuts that they brought with them on the caravan.
When they could, they ate small pieces of dry cured meat they had
brought along too. The voyage took months and was arduous.*

*They decided to settle high in the Atlas Mountains in what we
call Morocco today. The mountain (Jbel) they chose had streams
and an oasis. There was already a small settlement there, and they
welcomed everyone who would help them tame the land.*

*Now it's been thousands of years since my family arrived to
this mountain, and we feel like we are a part of it. My name is
Moses and my father's name was David, his father's name was
Moses and we go back like that until the beginning of time. We
are born out of this land. The trees know us, the grass knows us,
the streams know us, the rocks know us. We are as much a part
of this mountain as they are.*

*When the Pomegranate came to the middle of the Desert, I
could sense a difference in the air. This red juicy fruit was hardly
ever found in our vicinity. We usually had prickly desert fruits. We
also had date palms. But pomegranate trees? Not one could be*

54

found for miles and miles. This was a lost memory from the time when our family lived in the land of Israel.

I first heard about the Pomegranate from a Tuareg man called Mohammed who came to the Mountain. He had crossed the Desert and stopped at an oasis on the desert floor before coming up the Mountain. It was there that he heard about the magical Pomegranate. In the center of a tent hung with animal skins and women's woven carpets there was a gleaming red fruit. People said it could make 613 miracles, one for each of its seeds. Mohammed, dressed in his flowing blue robes and blue turban had gazed at the fruit and understood its value immediately. He was one of the many Muslims of this land who knew about Jewish traditions because he and his family had been intertwined with our history for years.

Meanwhile, I was on the Mountain, wondering what the new feeling in the air was all about.

The storyteller paused for a minute, taking a sip from his mint tea and clearing his throat. Everyone shifted, people coughed, I murmured a question to my neighbor—so, what would you ask for?

That evening Mohammed came to see me. He said he wanted to buy some spices from us. We sat quietly on the carpets we had laid outside the house. It was a clear starry night, and I asked him to tell me about his latest adventures through the Desert. I saw him twice a year, and he usually had at least one or two good stories to tell. Camels, trade routes, oasis gossip, weather patterns and of course we always talked politics.

This time though, he was unusually quiet. I knew there was something on his mind, and he would tell me when he had finished turning it around in his head.

We had a late meal in a large dish we shared. We balled up the food in our fingers and popped the delicious morsels of couscous, meat and vegetables and later washed it all down with tea.

Mohammed started telling me of a girl he had seen. Her name was Leila. She was veiled so he couldn't see her face, but her black sparkling eyes had spoken to him. It was her eyes that had stayed with him. They were rimmed in kohl and they flashed into him when he saw her. Leila's brother was Mohammed's brother-in-law. His sister was married to her brother. He had first seen her at their wedding. But this wasn't what was making his mind turn that night.

In the quiet silence of the Desert one becomes attuned to shifts, changes, movements and sounds. He was sitting there, slowly taking in the milky swath of stars that conglomerates in the night sky when there is no city for hundreds of miles. And he seemed to be appraising the rate of change in the stars tonight as compared to other nights in the past.

I couldn't understand why Mohammed would want to do this, but it seemed to me that it was related to the thought he kept on turning around in his mind that he was still not ready to speak about. Patiently, I waited.

Mohammed started speaking about the possibility of time expanding and contracting according to our perception of it.

I agreed! Isn't it interesting how sometimes time flies by and other times when you're bored it inches by millisecond by millisecond? Mohammed said that time actually does change, that it is a lot more malleable than what we think. Time can actually be shrunken, stretched, shortened and manipulated. When we know how to do this then we can understand how to be masters of the limitless. We can mold time like a ball, in our hands. It is a lie that has been taught to us that we are limited by time, that we are slaves of time.

'But how can I break out of the idea that constricts my mind into thinking that I am limited by time,' I asked Mohammed.

This is when he looked at me with a glint in his eye.

What secret would the storyteller tell us? I had heard about this storyteller and the magical power in his tales. People said that when you listened to his stories whatever happened to the characters would actually happen to you too. Could I learn how to mold time like a ball in my hand? I looked outside the small circle that had formed around the storyteller. There were hundreds of people, but only a precious few of us would hear his secrets and be transformed. Like with any mystical transformation, it usually happens in full view of others who can't see it.

Mohammed said that the world is a combination of lines and circles. It's how we combine the lines and circles that moves us forward, or makes us stagnant. This is how people survive when they cross the Desert. The Desert is one long line. The Mountain is another line but going perpendicular to the Desert. In this part of the world, we are surrounded by lines.

He continued, 'I saw an amazing circle in the heart of the Desert, a red juicy fruity circle. I understood that this Pomegranate is the secret to breaking open the boundaries of time. This circle is full of smaller circles. It has four circles within the One. The red outer cover, then a white inner filmy cover, then a red meaty juicy cover, and finally the circle of the seed itself.'

I realized that four stands for the four directions: North, South, East, West. So, within these four circles, there are also four lines: the directional lines. And if we add the four circles and the four lines together we have the number eight. In Judaism eight is the number that symbolizes anything that is above or beyond nature. Seven is the weekly cycle and the symbol of the natural order of things, eight is one beyond that, going beyond that artificial box of time we call the week. That is the space where we can mold time. How could we own the power of the circles and lines that intertwine in the pomegranate?

We could go to the tent and take a seed, or more than one seed, or the whole fruit. Mohammed wasn't sure what to do.

To own the power of molding time was almost too good to be true, and it seemed like having the magical power of the pomegranate seeds would help me mold time! The voices of desire and power spoke in my head struggling to control my thoughts. I started to picture how I could control my future and that of those around me if I were master of the limitless. Desire and excitement welled up in me and threatened to destroy the inner peace for which I have always felt grateful.

Then, I heard the voice of the Mountain.

'Come on Moshe, who are you kidding? I have lines and circles too; I am a line up from the desert; however every particle of dirt on me is a circle. Billions of small circles stacked on each other make me into a powerful mountain. Maybe all the billions of circles that form me also add up to One.'

Then I heard the rumbling of the Desert.

'Moshe, just be. I am also a line made of sand circles. You, Moshe, are a line made of lines and circles. If you can internalize the essence of circle and the essence of line, you will have access to the wisdom in all lines and circles. You won't need to possess any single thing in the world, not even the most magical seeds of the red juicy pomegranate to be able to control or mold time. It is all inside of you. You must go deeply into yourself and be the essence of line and be the essence of circle. You will then understand the pomegranate's mystical power, and you will be master of time.'

The storyteller had picked up his speed, the intervals of his inflections were wider and the flash in his eyes had intensified. I felt that I had been spun tightly into his story-web, and I promised myself to just be and meditate on the lines and circles that are me. Maybe I too could merit being a master of time.

Then, I heard the sweet soaring voice of the Pomegranate.

'Moshe, your ancestors all knew the secret of the pomegranate's lines and circles. You have it inscribed in your bones and sinews.

That was the most precious secret they carried from the Holy Land across the Desert to the Mountain. It was the mysterious mystical knowledge that the Jews brought to the Maghreb after the Destruction of the Temple.'

I looked over to where Mohammed was sitting, still observing the stars in the wide night sky. He looked over to me, and we both understood that we would be masters of time. But we would only be granted that gift if we understood how to feel that we were the smallest particle in creation. Only by complete humility and self-nullification would we be able to enter time. This was the secret knowledge locked in the seeds of the Pomegranate.

59

The storyteller's voice had dropped to a whisper. People dropped coins in a basket at his feet and quickly dispersed. There was a small breeze touching my cheeks, I walked towards the food carts and stopped to get a bag of toasted melon seeds. I couldn't hear the roar of people, music and activity at *Jama el Fna* tonight. I sat at a café to sip tea and felt myself disappear, sucked into the tea glass.

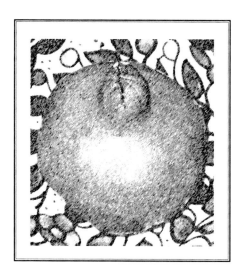

60

Estrella's prayers

In a mountainous town facing the Mediterranean sea, Estrella lived in a house at the top of a hill. The little house was a tower. It had only one room per floor and it shot straight up like a beacon of light towards the town.

Its little windows shone like stars out into the dark night, and during the day the blue-ness of the ocean and the sky flowed into the house. Sometimes little birds would fly inside chirping songs with secrets that Estrella knew how to decode and would then tell the people of her town. Maybe it was because her name means star, she had always felt an affinity with birds, the sky, the wind and basically anything that was in the air.

On the third floor of the house there was a little porch that led out to a garden. The garden was built into an ancient Portuguese wall that was 400 years old. There were plants, flowers and herbs, and doves and seagulls came to visit the little garden. Estrella always had breakfast in the garden and an occasional cup of tea, and as she sat there she frequently heard the call of the *muezzin* floating over the city.

Estrella's Jewish ancestors had come to this city hundreds of years before, traveling just across the Mediterranean Sea when the Spanish Kings decided only Catholics could live in Spain. There was even a beach that was called *Playa de los Judíos* (Beach of the Jews), where legend has it, the exiled Spanish Jews disembarked to rebuild their lives in Africa.

This town had been a haven for people from all over the world. There was every kind of religion, language, money and government. Every country that wanted could come and have their part of this town, and it came to be called the International Zone. There were English, French, Dutch, Portuguese, Spanish, German, American and many other nationalities that had an official presence. Large international populations enjoyed the openness of the town.

Estrella's neighbor was a single older Muslim man, who always had great home remedies for any ailment she or any one on their little street had. He was really a Sufi mystic, even though he didn't tell people he was. But, that's the way with most really spiritual people, they don't go around showing how deep they are, they just are. If you have the eyes to see it, then you do. If not, you think they are ordinary people like anyone else.

The daily market was at street level at the bottom of the Portuguese wall. When she needed fruits, vegetables, milk, farm eggs or, really anything, she would walk down the windy streets that led from the tower and the steps that led to the market. If she left early enough in the morning the streets were still wet from their early-morning washing, and sometimes when she was lucky, people had sprinkled rose water on the bricks to hide foul smells. When she walked on the rose-water splashed bricks she really felt like her day would be quite blessed.

In the *fondok* (market) she met Berber women who came to the town from the mountains of the Rif. They wore towels on their heads and a pom-pomed hat with a hand-woven striped red and white material tied as a skirt across their waist. These women, the *Jebliyas*, as people called them, came from the *Jbel* (mountain), and they spoke their own Berber language called *Riffi*. And they sold an amazingly delicious cheese wrapped in long fresh green leaves that were braided and circled around the cheese.

Estrella was the specialist in prayer in her town. People would come to her with all sorts of requests and wishes. Her prayers were powerful because she was always careful with her words. Since she took care of every word that came out of her mouth, she retained a special force in her words that other people had lost from too much talking or gossiping.

Estrella also had a unique gift of being able to reconnect backwards in time with the source-root of everything that had happened. So, if someone came to her with a concern about their health, she would go back in time to the root of that person's soul existence and see what imperfection, or wrinkle in their soul's creation was giving the present health problem.

How could she do this? She would focus all her thoughts on the person in front of her, she would doodle on a paper and draw whatever came to mind, she would write out the request, close her eyes, and travel into the energy-wave of non-existence and all-existence. Traveling into-beyond-through time, dispersing herself into a billion parts and into the One-ness of the Universe.

This is why she had to live in this town, where all the countries, languages and religions could exist peacefully. This was an embodiment of the Oneness of humanity, history and creation. In this kind of environment she could travel beyond time and into the deepest levels of the soul.

After each meeting, she would roll up the little paper she doodled on, and she would tie it to the branch of an olive tree at the entrance of the Jewish cemetery across from her tower. There had been so many people needing prayers throughout the years that the tree was full of floating papers that looked almost like another set of leaves. It was two trees in one, the prayer-paper tree and the olive tree. She had picked this tree because after the olives are crushed they give oil, which can become fire and light. Sometimes people need to be a little bit crushed so they can find their own light. Estrella prayed for people's light and hoped it would come without their being crushed.

One day when Estrella was in the *fondok* buying fresh mint for her tea, she saw a man that had a strange shadow hovering around him. That day it was a little harder than usual to re-connect backwards to the source-root when someone came requesting her prayer. She was a little surprised, but didn't make anything of it, thinking that maybe she wasn't rested enough or maybe she had done or said something to affect the purity of her soul. That would impede an easy connection.

The next day her Muslim Sufi neighbor confided in her that he had a very difficult night with terrible dreams, and he couldn't understand why. That morning they sipped a special tea he brewed and sat quietly in the garden. Later, she heard that the *Jbali* women hadn't come down from the mountains with their fresh cheeses on that day because there were shadowmen in their town. The Riffi people have always been very strong and proud. They would never come knowingly into a situation of physical vulnerability.

Estrella then understood that the man she had seen with the shadow hovering around him was one of them, and he had a dark energy accompanying him. These shadowmen were bringing seeds of separation and discord into their usually unified, peaceful town.

The town was flooded with shadowmen from all different countries, speaking all sorts of languages. They would sit in the sidewalk cafés, looking out on the street, observing and annotating details about people passing by. Townspeople began to be afraid of others, and they wouldn't confide in anyone outside of their close family. The birds and cats even seemed to become more aggressive with each other, and there seemed to be more storm clouds looming over the city with fewer sunny, warm breezy days.

Estrella lost her capacity of backward connecting in time. Daily life continued getting worse, and it had already been over a year since she had seen the first shadow-man that late morning in the market. Now she would walk through the *medina* streets on windy afternoons and see discarded papers swirling close to the ground. Many of the colorful shops had closed, people were quieter, there was less spontaneous drumming on the streets and less singing heard from the different halls of worship. There also were stinky piles of refuse on streets that used to be spic and span. Estrella became tired, bored and cranky. The paint was peeling off buildings that now looked dirty and decrepit. She felt dispirited. Her Sufi neighbor had left for a village in the South of the country—he said he would wait out the discord far away from the town and its unwelcome intruders.

Try as she might to say a prayer for the town, try as she might to connect backwards in time, Estrella's capacity for prayer seemed to be completely cut off. It felt almost as if she couldn't breath anymore. For her, praying was as integral to her life as breathing and speaking. She couldn't see the positive in anything anymore, and the days all looked gray and felt cold.

Estrella decided to go outside of the town to the mountains next to the Mediterranean Sea where the *Riffi* people lived. Since they had stopped coming into the town when the shadowmen were there, they retained their pure strength. She felt that hers had been zapped out of her. She packed some bread, dates and olives in a basket that she covered with a striped *Jbali* cloth and took a ride with a farmer who was leaving for the mountains that very afternoon. Once Estrella was of town, she started seeing the positive again. It was almost like disconnecting from the place of discord brought her back to connecting with unity.

They took the road that hugged the coast. It is quite a wonderful road with valleys that plunge deep down and mountains that jut upwards dramatically up out of the blue, peaceful sea. They passed some men that were wearing long gray tunics and yellow headpieces. This was the dress of the *Jbel*.

After driving for about forty-five minutes through the countryside, they arrived to the place where they were going, a small hill covered in yellow wildflowers that were swaying in the wind. Estrella could see some sheep grazing languidly and a young boy with a dog watching from under a tree, where he was protected from the sun. At the top of the hill there was a house surrounded with grape vines, and since it was early summer there were grape clusters dangling, almost asking to be picked.

She climbed to the top hill and knocked on the door. An older man opened, the wise *Riffi* man that she had heard about. He and his wife were a couple who knew how to deal with the vicissitudes of life. They gave advice to people from the entire region. Estrella had heard about them from her Sufi neighbor but had not come see them until now. When she spoke to them that afternoon over sweet mint tea she knew they had already heard about the problems in her town. She knew that they already knew about the shadowmen and the dark cloud that hung over them. But the words rippled and tumbled out of her as she exploded with feelings about the difficulties of the entire town. She felt like the town's soul had been kidnapped and that's why they weren't able to connect, pray and sing on those deeper levels anymore.

The wise *Riffi* couple told her that the people of the town would have to come together to fight this infiltration. It would not be possible to defeat the shadowmen with individual efforts. All the strands of people must come together and make their intention one. They must all focus on having their town restored to its former peace and its characteristic unification of opposites. The power of their unified intention would force the shadowmen out of their town.

Estrella pondered their method and realized the difficulty this solution presented. It would take a superhuman effort to bring all the different peoples together and to do it without the shadowmen sabotaging their plan. They would have to be discreet and swift.

She went back to her tower home with a renewed sense of duty in helping her town come through this difficult period. Estrella called for her Sufi neighbor from his refuge in the south. Once he came back they spoke and planned the gathering. They decided to convoke everyone for the evening of the next new moon.

During the next three days Estrella and her Sufi neighbor each went out and met with several heads of the different communities. They urged complete discretion about their gathering since the presence of just one of the shadowmen would ruin the whole thing.

As the new moon approached a sense of hushed expectation built in the town, it was as if everyone knew what was coming but the message was hanging silently in the air. People had been instructed to not talk about the gathering with absolutely anybody. Not even members of their own family. The message to attend was sent to each person through a secure method protected from the shadowmen. First each head of the community had a list of families who had always lived in the town. Plus they had methods of scanning if anyone had become a shadow-man. Of course, the foreign shadowmen were easy to detect, but others, which were infiltrated locals were more insidious and surprising to discover. This known, but unspoken secret, hung in everyone's minds and on everyone's lips.

66

The new moon finally arrived and the secret, not-so-secret gathering started unfolding. Slowly people from each of the different communities began to appear on the rooftop terraces of their houses. If they lived in a building without a rooftop terrace, they had been instructed to go to someone's house with a rooftop terrace. Slowly and consistently the terraces began filling up with smiling people. These people had defied the dark cloud hanging over the town and were beaming with the pleasure of accomplishment. The whole town was on the rooftop terraces, except for the shadowmen, that could be seen scurrying in the alleys, trying to take cover from the unveiled eyes of the people.

The sky was pink, yellow and cerulean blue. Estrella could see schools of birds flying high and the ocean was gray-blue, almost silver with foam ridges every once in a while. It was twilight on the evening of the new moon and everything seemed possible. There were people standing on the rooftops as far as the eye could see and everyone was smiling. Some voices broke out in a chant "We are one, we are one, we are one." Women wept with joy, children jumped up and down in their excitement and the whole population understood their own power to vanquish the elements of discord in their midst. The force of their unified intention shriveled up the influence from the invading elements of discord.

If only they had done this a long time ago!! But maybe, just maybe did they need to have those shadowmen come to remind them of the importance of their constant active affirmation of the unification of opposites. If the discord hadn't arisen, and their lives hadn't been interrupted in such an unpleasant manner they would not have appreciated and continued nurturing the special status of their town as International Zone, unique in the world as a place for the equal gathering of different peoples.

****

Life went back to its pleasant routine, the *Jbali* women came back into the town to sell their cheese, people resumed confiding in each other and Estrella regained her ability to reconnect backwards in time to the root of any present reality.

(Inspired in the city of Tangier and its history)

Zohra's Song

At the top of a towering tower-ous building in the shiny white North African city of Casablanca there was a little baby boy sleeping peacefully in a cocoon bed. He would sleep and dream of wonderful and exciting adventures that were happening hundreds of feet down at the noisy, smelly, gritty, grimy street level.

He was safely and warmly snuggled in his cocoon-bed in a room with windows in all directions. He could see the Atlantic Ocean and its foaming waves from his window. He could also see the old lighthouse the French built at the edge of the sea. During the day it was a white tower sticking up against the azure ocean but as soon as the sun set, its shining greenish light flashed across the city into the window-room.

He could also see the huge mosque that the previous King had built to secure his immortality. It is the second largest mosque in the world and dwarfs every single thing in the cityscape. It is beautiful when the golden yellow glow sunset light hits it on clear evenings. He could see the sun rising as a red flaming ball appearing out of the city horizon when he woke up to have his warm milk-bottle in the morning. He could see seagulls and doves gliding on the wind-waves that rolled off the surface of the sea unto the city. He could also see the thousands of buildings surrounding his tower. Square ones, rectangular ones, large and small buildings with windows of every shape and size, minaret towers with arched windows and terraces. Terraces where people would hang their laundry or just set up their satellite dishes so they could have messages sent to them from around the world. Tiled terraces where people had plants and chairs and tables, carpets and bird baths. Terraces where sometimes women would gather to talk to their neighbors from rooftop to rooftop, also wanting to catch a glimpse down at the city from this birds-eye view, the gleaming white shiny city seen from above.

In this window-room at the top of the city of Casablanca where the little baby boy slept peacefully there was also a gecko hiding out from the rain and wind that this year's winter had brought to the coastal African city. The gecko first shyly appeared one afternoon when the parents' discussion was about the new kitchen tiles. She was hanging upside down from the ceiling with her toes glued to the plaster ceiling. NOT MOVING at all...somehow she figured, if she didn't move they wouldn't see her. Never mind that she was a dark green lizard-type creature and the ceiling was painted white...

When Zohra, the gecko realized that the mother had seen her but had not panicked or tried to drive her from the tower window-room, she got very excited and in her lizard way, she ran across the ceiling to explore the tower window-room from another perspective.

The next day she was at the other corner of the ceiling, and quite amazed to be out in the open with humans, and with a BABY sleeping peacefully in a cocoon bed. Maybe if she made some of her chirping mating sounds they would think she's a bird? She decided against it, and thought it would be too risqué to not only show herself, but also sing for them.

The third appearance she made was some days later, she was on the wall by the window to the sea. This time she decided to face down, towards them and get a good look at what it is that happens in the world of humans, but this change of direction seemed to have provoked much consternation. The mother was fluttering around the room with a camera, taking picture after picture of her. By this time she realized, either she established a relationship with them, or she would have to go back into hiding from the world of humans. They seemed to see her as an exotic addition to their lives, and not just as the plain old gecko that she, Zohra the gecko, felt herself to be. She could not live this way.

She asked herself, why is it that always when we are faced with something different from what we expect it to be, we separate ourselves from it and exoticize it? Why is it that the unexpected becomes so fascinating? She didn't want to be exoticized or fascinating because she was a gecko in the window-room. She wanted to share the wonder of looking towards the ocean, the lighthouse, the mosque, the sunrise and the city, just like they did, even though they were humans, and she was Zohra the gecko.

Zohra was a little bit upset when she went to sleep that night. The mother had made such a big deal that she was on the wall looking down and not just a distant, outlandish addition to their ceiling...how would she ever be able to connect with them in a simple, normal way?

That night Zohra was quite restless, she had to come up with a way to get through to these humans without them always exoticizing her. The greenish light from the lighthouse flashed in from the windows while everyone slept in the next room. Zohra followed the light through the city and into the room...then she had an idea. She would send thought brain waves to the baby and see if they could communicate. It was too hard to do that with the adults. Since adults speak human language they lose a sensibility that helps them communicate non-verbally. But, BUT the baby didn't speak yet! Maybe he would be able to communicate with Zohra and then he could one day remember what he had heard from the gecko! Zohra thought it was a great idea and was really quite excited about the prospect of some communication with a human.

The next morning Zohra decided this day was the day she would communicate with the baby through her brain waves. When the baby came into the window-room in the late morning and sat in his little hammock chair she started to send thoughts to him. She was sending thoughts about the temperature in the room, and the clear light of this morning, the fact it had thundered and rained during the night... and the baby, the baby responded! He sent her thoughts about the view from the window, the lighthouse and the sea, the mosque and the terraces, and all those thousands of white buildings.

Zohra got so excited! They were having a thought-conversation! And the baby didn't think it was weird to communicate with a gecko. In fact, he didn't even know, probably, because he had never communicated with a human through thoughts. Maybe he thought this was normal? The only sounds he knew how to make were ah-goo, ga, ma, and others like that. Which meant he wanted to say things but communication was still free; he was not yet tied into words and defined thoughts.

That evening the baby was lying on his cocoon sleeping and Zohra started approaching him. She wanted to whisper into his ear some of the secrets of the city. She knew that the baby must have dreamed about what he saw outside; the street with its noise, grit and grime were mysterious, foreboding and exciting. Zohra knew that such large buildings and so many cars seemed scary, and from the tower window-room it was all distant and difficult to understand.

This time she was on the other side of the room, again facing down on a red wall that had a large painting and the sofa at the bottom. This is where the baby was sleeping on his cocoon bed. Zohra started the trek down the window-room's red wall—here she was green gecko splat spread out on the wall, and the baby sleeping peacefully in a sky-blue puffy fluffy blanket surrounding the cocoon.

Then Zohra decided that she didn't really need to whisper into his ear, since they had already established their thought form of communication. And, actually, maybe the baby would not know how to understand the whispers...he understood the thoughts, but maybe not the whispers.

Zohra hadn't really considered that possibility until now. She had gotten so excited once communication had been established that she let her imagination run. She was already planning on all sorts of things they could talk about. She was so excited because finally her dream of being able to communicate with a human without being exotic and bizarre had come true! She never imagined that it would be with a baby. But, of course, it made sense that this is the way it would be.

The baby woke up and was looking up toward the ceiling, but he couldn't see Zohra the gecko because the large painting of a Princess being serenaded in a garden was between the two of them. Zohra started think-talking with the baby telling him about the view from where she was and how the Moroccan lamps by the mother's desk made great light-patterns on the wall.

The baby agreed, those patterns were fascinating to him. He loved the patterns of light and shadow. Then, he started sending Zohra thoughts about his dreams about the city below, the horns and cars, the sirens, grime, and thousands and thousands of buildings. He thought to Zohra that he was excited about exploring all those things below but he was also afraid. He didn't really understand so many buildings, streets, cars, trucks, motorcycles, bicycles, horse-driven carts, donkey-driven carts, and of course, people.

Zohra realized that it was difficult to get her thoughts across like this. So, she started descending toward the baby so she could whisper her advice into his ear. But she was afraid, because the baby's mother was just across the room, working on the computer, and she might freak out and take the baby away.

When the mother walked out of the room, Zohra gained courage and walked closer to the baby.

When she found herself behind the painting of the princess being serenaded, she had a flash of inspiration, she should sing for him! The painting had the special quality of inviting people and even geckos to sing what they had to say. Zohra was worried that the mother would walk back into the room, so she held herself back a little and then realized that the mother might think that the song was coming from the painting itself. Not a bad thing!

So Zohra began singing. She sang (in her chirpy gecko voice) the songs she had heard from her mother. She sang about the beautiful shiny city gleaming white against the Atlantic Ocean. She sang that although everything seems like it's separated from everything else, actually they are all interconnected. She sang her gecko wisdom to him and he was enchanted. Zohra was happy that he had listened to her.

73

The baby was happy to have heard Zohra's song, and he understood that the city should not be as scary as he had once thought it to be. If it wasn't scary and foreboding from above, then it didn't have to be from below. He loved her singing chirpy voice and thought he would never forget it. He understood that he did not have to be afraid.

The next day was the Sabbath, and the baby left with his mother and father to visit his grandparents across town, next to the ocean. That rainy Sabbath afternoon Zohra disappeared and never came back to visit again.

(Inspired by real events that transpired with a gecko, a mother and a baby in a window-room in a tower in Casablanca on January 2010)

La Casa De Las Sereias

In a city on the banks of a river beautiful hills rose on both sides, and winding alleyways made mysterious passages from one world to another. From one side of the river you could look across and see the lights blinking at night on the other side, and in the daytime you saw the gleaming façades of the houses in white, touched by green, yellow, and blue.

At the top of one of these hills was a stunning house that belonged to a Jewish family. It was perched in such a spot that you could see the river and the boats floating at the wharfs, and you could also see out to the place where the river and the ocean waters met in the kiss of salty and sweet waters. It was a white three-story house with a big imposing door flanked by two gigantic stone sirens that upheld the door.

A girl named Mia lived in this house, and she walked in and out of the mermaid door everyday on her way to school. One day the sirens called her name "Mia" as she was arriving home. She was shocked that the statues spoke and asked them how they knew her name. They told her that they not only knew her name but also her grandmother's and her great-grandmother's names, and that there was a special secret they had to tell her. They had been waiting until she was old enough to understand and do what it required. She had no idea what they were talking about, but it sounded so interesting, so she asked them what was the secret?

They told her they would only tell her if she would promise to complete the task that they would ask of her. She thought about it for a while and agreed that she would to do it.

The Sirens told Mia that there was a secret passageway some-where in the house and her task was to find it. Then she had to enter it and find the next step.

As soon as she went in the house, she started looking for a passageway in all the different rooms. She looked in her closet, in her mother's closet, in the bathroom, in the cellar and in the kitchen. Finally, when she looked under the kitchen sink, she noticed a panel of wood on the back wall, and as she pulled it off, she saw a passageway with descending stairs. Mia squirmed her way into the passageway, which was tight at first, and then discovered that it became larger and larger and with a higher and higher vaulted roof and at the end of this hallway there was a door that opened to a small room.

Inside the room Mia found a letter addressed to her with a golden key. The letter told her that she was chosen as a leader of her people, and that she had to find the jeweled chest with help of a fisherman called Danny.

She came out of the passageway with the key and the letter and by the time she was back in the house, it was time for dinner. She really wanted to tell the Sirens of her success, but now she would have to wait until the next morning. That night Mia dreamed that she was swimming in the ocean with the Sirens, and they were speaking to her underwater about all sorts of wonderful secrets. First thing in the morning Mia went out to speak with the Sirens. They were thrilled to learn of her success in having found the passageway and the key to unlock her secret gift.

Mia didn't know where to find Danny the fisherman, so she asked the Sirens where she should start looking for him. They told her to go to the fish market down by the river and ask for Danny and then everything would be clear.

The next day after school, Mia went straight to the fish market with the key and the letter buried deep in her book bag. The fishmongers were arranged in long hallways on a small incline with all their fresh fish laid out on ice inside of new hand-made wicker baskets. Some of them had tiled counters with fish all lined up and others were cleaning and de-boning the fish for customers. There was water running down the incline as the fishmongers cleaned off their fish, and people were shouting all sorts of fish names and fish prices. Mia had never been here, it was so interesting and full of action! She started asking people where she could find Danny the fisherman and after only asking three people someone pointed her in the right direction.

When Mia walked up to Danny the fisherman, she noticed that his eyes were very gentle, and he seemed like he was beyond time. She couldn't really figure out how old he was, he was one of those ageless people. He had baggy pants and a loose cotton shirt, and he looked right at her and said, "Wait here until I'm done, and then we'll go."

Mia sat down next to Danny's fish stand and watched all that was happening in the market. After a half hour or so Danny came over to her and said, "OK let's go."

They walked down toward the docks where all the boats waited patiently for their masters to float out into the middle of the waters. If they were lucky, they went out to the Ocean. Danny was easy going and he told Mia that he knew her mother and grandmother very well. Mia wondered if he had ever heard the Sirens speaking.

Danny said to Mia "I know that you have a special task to complete. Your grandmother told me many years ago that you would come to look for me some day. Once you came your destiny would start to unfold and my part in the puzzle is to take you out on my boat to a place you will indicate. If you are ready for your task, you will know how to pick the right place." Now all of a sudden Mia got nervous. What if she picked the wrong spot? What would happen then? But then she looked at Danny, and his serene eyes calmed her down. She knew that she would know the right place.

They went out on the boat into the center of the calm waters of the bay, and Mia felt the pull of the currents as they moved slowly towards the ocean. Mia felt a great sense of peace. Suddenly she asked Danny to stop, they had reached the spot she felt was right. He dropped the anchor. They were at the point of confluence between the river and the ocean.

Mia started to pray and asked to be ready to receive the message that the Sirens had sent her to retrieve. They sent a hook down into the waters and waited to see if anything happened. They waited. The sun was hiding behind the clouds, it was one of those days with a lot of light but no sun. It was a gray whitish kind of day.

In one instant when a feeling of futility was beginning to creep into Mia's mind everything completely changed. She felt a tug on the line, and they started to reel it up. It was heavy and came from deep waters. When it came up to the surface, she gasped at the beauty of the chest that she saw. She pulled the key out of her bag and shaking with excitement put the key in the keyhole.

Opening the treasure chest, she found beautiful jewels, and each of these pieces had special powers. When she wore one, her vision of the depth and beauty of people became more refined. When she wore another one, she perceived the suffering and weakness of others with more acuity. With yet a different one, she could understand what the truth was behind a mysterious situation.

But the only reason the jewels had this effect was because Mia was the person that was supposed to wear them. She knew how to use these jewels to help her people live a happier and more fulfilling life.

She was the heiress of this tradition that had been locked away for many years waiting for her to be ready to accept her position and responsibility.

Danny took her back to the shore, and Mia found a special gift in the box for him. He did not want to accept anything because for him it was enough to have helped Mia find her destiny. She told him she wanted him to accept it, so he and his family could live an easier life, he could sell the jewel and buy a house overlooking the bay.

Mia went back home and told the Sirens about the beauty of Danny, the jewels and her experience unlocking the secret of her destiny. They were so happy and proud of her achievement and the courage to discover and fulfill herself.

Word started spreading around the city that finally the tradition of the visionary woman had been restored to their city. People would line up to go into the *Casa de las Sereias* to see Mia and be touched by her great wisdom and inner peace. People that felt lost started to find their way. Everyone was inspired by this young girl's insight into the truths of life, and the whole city was restored to glory and goodness. Difficult situations were handled with compassion and understanding, and people started to open their hearts and minds to one another. Mia continued helping and being a healer for her people, she grew up, got married and had a wonderful husband. They had many children that ran through the yards and played games of mystery and fantasy, always knowing that their mother had been a girl who followed her dreams and had the courage to take risks that led her to be the great woman she was.

81

Epilogue

Life is One 83

In Morocco and beyond the *muezzin* begins the day with the call to prayer; Muslims kneel and genuflect, Jewish don tefillin and prayer shawls, Christians bow their heads, Madame Soulika pounds the bread dough for the day, a gecko comes out of its hiding place to watch the humans, babies are fed, songs are sung, and stories are told.

The great circle of life turns another day.

Glossary

Atlas Mountains -- A mountain chain between Morocco and Algeria.

Baraka -- Arabic word for blessing.

Bechor -- Hebrew word for first born son.

Berber -- The original tribal inhabitants of Morocco, and the Atlas Mountains are their traditional home.

Boteroesque -- Voluminous figures (style of Colombian painter Botero)

Cantigas D'Amigo -- A cycle of love songs from Medieval Portugal.

Carroza -- Arabic word for cart or large wheelbarrow.

Dome of the Rock -- The gold domed building on the Temple Mount in Jerusalem that covers the rock which has been attributed as the place on which Abraham performed the binding of Isaac, on which Jacob slept when he had his dream of the ladder ascending to heaven, and from which Mohammed ascended to heaven.

Djama el Fna -- The central square of the old city of Marrakesh.

Djellaba -- The traditional robe-like Moroccan garment with a hood.

Estrella -- Spanish for star.

Falafel -- Traditional Middle-Eastern chick pea patties which are deep fried.

F'Kan Kohen -- Judeo-Arabic for redeeming of the firstborn.

Fondok -- Market.

Fundador -- Spanish for founder, i.e founder of a city.

Geffen -- Hebrew word for wine.

Gnawa musicians -- Former sub-Saharan African slave-musicians from a Sufi brotherhood that practice trance-healing ceremonies. Today they frequently perform in public spaces in Morocco to earn a living.

Haketía -- Moroccan Judeo-Spanish. A language that combines medieval Spanish, Hebrew, and Moroccan Arabic.

Hallah bread -- The traditional bread eaten on the Jewish Sabbath.

Hammam -- Stream bath.

Harira -- Traditional Moroccan soup.

Jbali -- Berber for women.

Jbel -- Mountain or peak.

Jebliyah -- A Berber woman from the Rif Mountains in Northern Morocco.

Judería -- Spanish word for Jewish quarter.

Kohl -- Black eyeliner used by women.

Kohanim -- The plural of Kohen or Cohen in Hebrew, referring to descendents of the priestly class.

Kotel -- The Western Wall of the Temple in Jerusalem, which is a central place of prayer for Jews.

La Place -- French for square or plaza.

Mahane Yehuda shuk -- The traditional marketplace in West Jerusalem.

Mantilla -- Silk, embroidered shawl for women.

Medina -- Arabic word for city, which refers to a cluster of traditional houses built around the marketplace.

Mellah -- The word for Jewish quarter in Morocco. It comes from the Arabic word for salt, referring to the salting of meat. Jews were known for salting meat in the koshering process.

Muezzin -- The man who calls out the invitation to prayer five times each day at mosques.

Pañolón -- A woolen shawl used by women for warmth in the Andes Mountains of Colombia.

Paytanim -- Men who sing Hebrew liturgical poetry.

Plaza de mercado -- Spanish for outdoor marketplace.

Pidión HaBen -- Hebrew name for the ceremony to redeem the first-born male son.

Rahman -- Hebrew word for compassion.

Rehem -- Hebrew word for womb.

Rehmido -- Haketía word for redeeming of the first born, referring to the opening of the womb.

Riad -- A home with a courtyard in the old city or medina of Moroccan cities. Many have been restored as luxury boutique hotels.

Riffi people -- People from the Rif Mountains in Morocco, an extension of the Atlas Mountains.

Sereias -- Sirens.

Shuk -- Marketplace.

Sufi -- A practitioner of mystical Islam.

Tajine -- Traditional Moroccan meal.

Tangerine -- A person who lives in Tangier.

Tefillin -- Small boxes containing prayer scrolls that are bound to the arm and forehead during morning prayers in the Jewish tradition.

Tuareg -- A nomadic group in the Sahara known for their blue robes and elaborate jewelry.

Kol Bat Series
Gaon Books

Voices of Jewish Women
Vanessa Paloma, Editor

Kol Bat (voice of the daughter) is the mirror image of the Biblical phrase Bat Kol, which refers to the echo of a feminine voice responding to unanswerable questions from the heavens. Through this collection, contemporary women speak with insightful voices in the worlds of academia, religion, activism, arts and beyond.

Titles

Volume 1. Nina S. de Friedemann.
African Saga: Cultural Heritage and Resistance in the Diaspora.
2007.

Volume 2. Vanessa Paloma.
Mystic Siren: Woman's Voice in the Balance of Creation. 2007.

Volume 3. Silvia Hamui Sutton.
Cantos judeo-españoles: simbología poética y visión del mundo. 2008.

Volume 4. Susan Vorhand.
The Mosaic Within: An Alchemy of Healing Self and Soul. 2009.

Volume 5. Angelina Muñiz-Huberman.
The Confidantes. 2009.

Volume 6. Isabelle Medina-Sandoval.
Guardians of Hidden Traditions. 2009.

Volume 7. Carol Rachlin.
Seasons of Rita: the Biography of a Sauk Indian Woman. 2010.

Volume 8. Rabbi Min Kantrowitz.
Counting the Omer: A Kabbalistic Meditation Guide. 2010.

Volume 9. Sandra K. Toro
By Fire Possessed: Doña Gracia Nasi. 2010.

Volume 10. Patricia Gottlieb Shapiro.
Coming Home to Yourself: Eighteen Wise Women Reflect on their Journeys. 2010.

Volume 11. Vanessa Paloma.
The Mountain, the Desert, and the Pomegranate: Stories from Morocco and Beyond. 2011.

Volume 12. Anne Freeling Schlezinger.
Pulling It All Together: Diaries by One of America's First Jewish Women Judges. 2011.

Forthcoming:

Volume 13. Isabelle Medina-Sandoval.
Grandmother's Secrets. 2011.

Volume 14. Sandra K. Toro. *Princes, Popes and Pirates.* 2011.

Volume 15. Estrella Jalfón de Bentolila.
Haketía: Judeo-Spanish Language and Culture from Morocco. 2011.

Volume 16. Susana Weich-Shahak.
The Sephardic Romancero from Morocco. 2011.

Volume 17. Gloria Abella Ballen.
The Power of the Hebrew Alphabet.

Published in collaboration with
Gaon Institute
A 501 c 3 organization that supports
tolerance through literacy.
www.gaoninstitute.org